DMITRI
THE ASTRONAUT

STORY AND PICTURES BY JON AGEE

Michael di Capua Books

HarperCollins Publishers

IT WAS JUST BEFORE DAWN

when Dmitri the astronaut touched down in the Atlantic Ocean. He'd been on the moon for two and a half years, collecting rocks.

His mission was complete.

An early riser on the *S.S. Knickerbocker* spotted the strange castaway.

"Who are you?" the Captain asked.

"I'm Dmitri the astronaut!"

"Never heard of you," said the Captain. "But welcome aboard my ship."

Dmitri hardly had a chance to relax before some-
body recognized him.

"Aren't you Barney Abernathy from Cincinnati?"

"No!" said Dmitri. "I'm Dmitri the astronaut!"

"Oh," said the man, "I'm so sorry."

When the ship docked in New York, Dmitri headed straight for Times Square.

"It's me, Dmitri the astronaut!" he shouted. "I'm back from the moon!"

"Beat it, buddy," said a hot-dog vendor.

"That's funny," thought Dmitri. "Nobody remembers me."

He decided to visit the Museum of Intergalactic Exploration. Surely they'd know him there.

The main exhibition had changed while he was gone.
Dmitri was impressed.

His next stop was the moon display.

"Oh, dear!" he said.

Dmitri was crushed.

"I guess I was up on the moon too long," he said.
"That's why nobody remembers me."

Dmitri dumped his sack of moon rocks in the trash
and wandered away.

But there was something else in the sack.

Dr. Geoffrey W. Beaton, the Nobel Prize—winning naturalist, almost fell off his bike.

"What a peculiar creature!" he said. "Come along, I'm taking you to the Academy of Science."

The scientists had never seen a specimen like this before. They were particularly struck by its flair for drawing.

"My dear colleagues," Dr. Beaton announced, "we must tell the world of my amazing discovery. There's no time to waste!"

The next day, Dmitri happened to be passing the Academy.

Those polka dots looked extremely familiar. "Lulu?" said Dmitri. "Is that *you*?"

When he finally got close enough, there was no doubt about it. *"Lulu!"* cried Dmitri. "Oh, Lulu!"

"What's going on here?" Dr. Beaton demanded.

"This is Lulu," said Dmitri, "my old pal from the moon."

"The moon? Good heavens!" said Dr. Beaton. "You wouldn't be that astronaut . . . Dim . . . Dim . . ."

"Dmitri!" said Dmitri.

"Why, of course! It's Dmitri the astronaut!"

Dmitri was so happy. The world remembered him after all.

"By the way, Lulu," he said, "how'd you get here?"